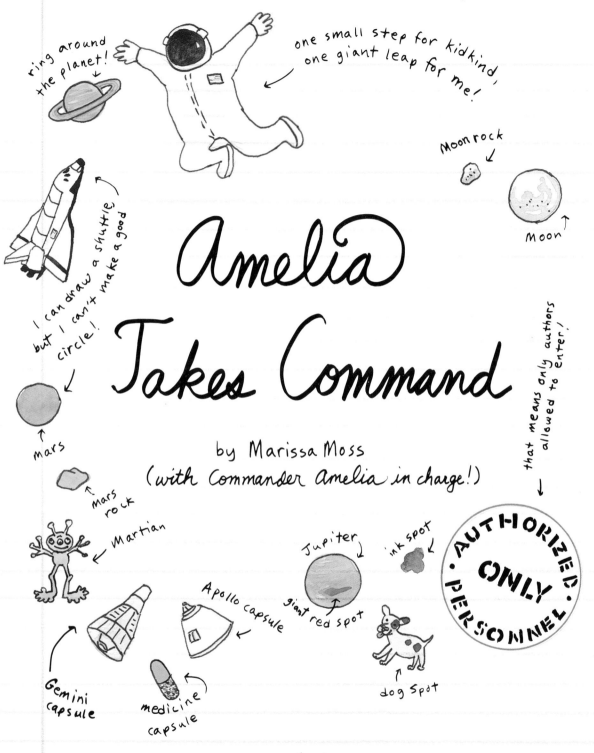

ring around the planet!

one small step for kidkind, one giant leap for me!

Moon rock

Moon

I can draw a shuttle but I can't make a good circle!

# Amelia Takes Command

by Marissa Moss
(with Commander Amelia in charge!)

that means only authors allowed to enter!

mars

mars rock

Martian

Jupiter

giant red spot

ink spot

AUTHORIZED ONLY · PERSONNEL

Apollo capsule

Gemini capsule

medicine capsule

dog Spot

American Girl

This notebook is dedicated to
Nicole Geiger,
a truly super editor

new 5th grade backpack

lanyard I made on the zipper

official-sounding yada yada yada

this means kids have to write their own notebooks!

Pleasant Company
Publications
8400 Fairway Place
Middleton, Wisconsin
53562

Book Design by Amelia

Library of Congress Cataloging-in-Publication Data
Moss, Marissa
Amelia takes command / by Marissa Moss
p. cm.
Summary: After successfully commanding the Discovery shuttle mission at Space Camp, Amelia returns to fifth grade where she deals with the bully who has been making her life miserable.
ISBN 1-56247-789-7   ISBN 1-56247-788-9 (pbk.)
[1. Bullies—Fiction  2. Teasing—Fiction  3. Camps—Fiction
4. Schools—Fiction  5. Diaries—Fiction  I. Title]
PZ7. M8535Ai 1999                                    98-40672
[Fic]--dc21                                              CIP
                                                          AC

now I ride a BIG bicycle!

Originally published by Tricycle Press
First Pleasant Company Publications printing, 1999

An Amelia™ Book
American Girl™ is a trademark of Pleasant Company.
Amelia™ and the black-and-white notebook pattern
are trademarks of Marissa Moss.

elevator going up

Manufactured in Singapore

secret codes for secret agents

99 00 01 02 03 04 TWP 10 9 8 7 6 5 4 3

I love getting school supplies!

← new pencils – sharp, sharp, sharp – with that great new pencil smell

fresh, clean, pink erasers (I wish they could stay this way, but I know they'll get all smudgy.)

new school clothes →

new shoes with clean white soles and laces →

Tomorrow is my first day as a fifth grader. (I **love** that sentence – I'm a 5th GRADER!)

Leah has already planned what she's wearing and what's going to be in her lunch. I'm just planning on being excited – and a little nervous. I wonder what my new teacher will be like. Will I like the other kids? Will they like me? Leah's not in my class, but I can still see her at lunch and recess.

great new binder with lots of pockets and dividers because now I'm in 5th grade and I'll need those things

Leah is **so** organized, she even knows which barrettes she'll wear (but then, she **folds** her underwear before putting it away)

my dresser drawer

Leah's dresser drawer

Well, now I know what my teacher is like, and I wish I didn't. Leah gets the good 5th grade teacher, Mr. Reyes – he brought in cookies for the whole class on the first day. I get the witch, Ms. Busby. The first thing she did was read all these rules to us.

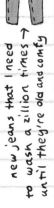

new jeans that I need to wash a zillion times until they're old and comfy →

Ms. Busby →

eyebrows that mean business —

mouth pinched tight —

loooong list of rules —

su
top o
If you
have to
over ag
If your
completed
after scho
That is a c
We are her
means trea
with courte
no teasing,
no name-c
no shoutin
Every tin
by your
When
th

mayonnaise gooing up everything ↘

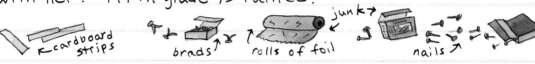

dizzzguzzzting! ↖!

← I didn't even have a decent lunch on the first day — Mom put mayonnaise on my baloney sandwich by mistake — I <u>hate</u> mayonnaise! (I even hate spelling it!)

frog

Raoul brought his pet frog the first day.

She's not like my old teacher at all. A whole year with her! Fifth grade is ruined!

 ← cardboard strips     brads ↗    rolls of foil    junk ↗    nails ↗

Hilary might be friendly. I like her smile.

Maya's voice is so soft, you can barely hear it.

I don't even like the classroom. There are boxes of junk blocking the bookshelf. Bits of wood, wire, and nails — it looks like Cleo's room in here! (Only with Cleo the mess is made of soda cans, empty nail polish bottles, pretzel and chip crumbs, and dirty socks.) What's all that stuff <u>for</u> anyway? I bet Ms. Busby is going to build some kind of torture device. It's torture enough just going to school. We never get to do ANYTHING fun! Plus it's hard not having Leah in the same class. None of the other kids is nice to me. Well, Jacqueline is a little friendly, but I can tell she really likes Susie — she's just polite to me. This year is the worst!

Luis skate-boards to school — lucky!

Jacqueline just moved here from Arkansas — I love her accent!

Franny (or is it Amy? I can never tell those twins apart) ↗

Max →

Of all the kids in the class, I only know Franny and Max.

Susie already raises her hand <u>every</u> time!

Jon hasn't said one word yet, except "Here."

Charlie fell asleep when the rules were read.

Ms. Busby says she's sorry to block the book-case, but she's collecting things for our first science project. I finally get to 5th grade and it's like I'm back in kindergarten, hammering nails into wood and calling it sculpture.

Gabe always has his nose in a book.

Carly seems the shyest.

Lucy and Matilda must be best friends — they whisper together CONSTANTLY!

Seth keeps sneaking snacks- he smells like popcorn.

ooooh! what beautiful art!

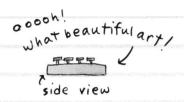

↑ side view

top view →

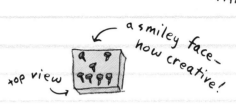

a smiley face- how creative!

All that junk turned out to be not so junky. We put it all together and made a telegraph. It was so000 cool! I wrote to Nadia and drew her a picture so she can make her own. I wish we could tap out messages to each other, but I don't have a long enough wire.

Brandon jiggles his foot all the time — it's driving me crazy!

I LOVE making inventions.

tap this down and then the brad taps the nail, making a clicking sound

cardboard taped down

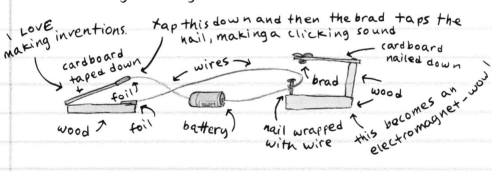

wires →

← brad

cardboard nailed down

← wood

this becomes an electromagnet—wow!

wood ↗   foil

battery

nail wrapped with wire

It would have been a perfect day, but at recess, Leah didn't play with me. She was too busy jumping rope with Gwen, some girl in her class. I looked for someone I could jump rope with, but everyone already has a friend (except Hilary — she was swinging on the bars and I didn't want to do that).

I guess this notebook is kind of like having a friend — it listens to what I have to say. But it doesn't talk back to me (at least we can't fight that way).

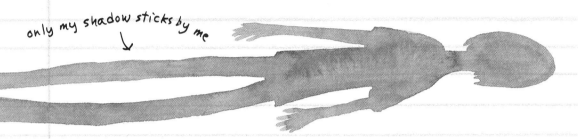

eyebrows that are happy →

← head full of good ideas

friendly smiling mouth →

At least now I like Ms. Busby — she's still strict, but she has good ideas for projects. She says we'll make rockets next! And she <u>can</u> be funny — she's just serious about learning. That's ok — when she does smile, it's great!

Leah won't walk to school with me anymore! She walks with Gwen instead. Just when I start to like school, something rotten happens.

only my shadow sticks by me ↓

Would I look better with hair like this? ↓

or this? ↓

or this? ↓

How about a fancy chocolate chip hairdo? )

↑ the problem is, none of these look like ME!

I really need a friend now, a close-by friend, not a far-away friend like Nadia. I can't believe I ever thought Hilary might be friendly — she's mean, <u>mean</u>, <u>MEAN</u>! She said I look like a doofus because I don't wear knee socks and I have a stupid haircut. What's wrong with my hair and why does it matter what kind of socks I wear? But once she said it, everyone else started believing it. Lucy and Matilda wouldn't play four-square with me and when I sat down next to Susie at lunch, she changed places. It was awful.

I <u>knew</u> this would be the worst year of my life!

Hilary said my hair looks like a mop and I should wash the floor with it. Then she tried to trip me. I wanted to cry, but no <u>way</u> would I EVER let her see me cry.

bathroom mirror

sink ↓

I looked in the mirror for so long my face didn't look like me anymore.

Cleo has one tough punch

Mom says to pretend I can't hear what Hilary says — but I hear all the mean things she says too well!

Everyone says you should just ignore teasing and it will go away, but it's <u>not</u> going away. I try to pretend I'm a stone when Hilary talks to me, but inside I feel like I'm crumbling. Why doesn't Leah like me anymore, either? Have I changed somehow? Do I have B.O.?

bad socks D−

do socks really matter?

good socks A+

now Hilary says my new shoes are dumb — turns out they're the <u>wrong</u> brand!

I called Leah on the phone and asked what's wrong. She said nothing's wrong, she <u>still</u> likes me, but she's so busy with Gwen, she doesn't have time for <u>2</u> friends. Of course, she picks the person in the same class as her (and Gwen wears <u>knee</u> socks!).

Maybe what I need is a good luck charm.

four-leaf clover

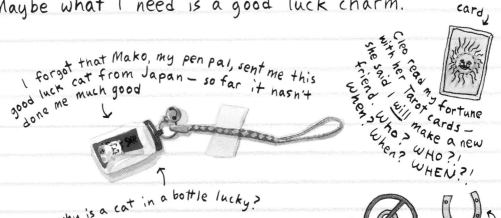

I forgot that Mako, my pen pal, sent me this good luck cat from Japan — so far it hasn't done me much good

why is a cat in a bottle lucky?

Tarot card

Cleo read my fortune with her Tarot cards — she said I will make a new friend. When? Who? WHO?! When? WHEN?!

rabbit's foot — very <u>unlucky</u> for the rabbit!

don't let your luck run out

horseshoe

We started the next science project today —

# ROCKETS!

Real ones, not just models. We're going to have a big launch day when we're done and see whose flies the best. We have to work with a partner and I held my breath, hoping, hoping, hoping Hilary would NOT be my partner. She's not! She's Seth's partner — what a relief!

Carly is my partner. She likes science as much as I do, and I saw she has a notebook in her desk — it looks like mine!

Carly's notebook ↘

she put stickers all over the cover →

the splotches are green, not black →

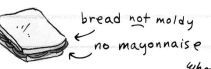

Today Hilary said my lunch looked gross. Now she's insulting my _food_. She's always looking for something mean to say.

innocent apple — no bruises or worms

bread _not_ moldy ←
no mayonnaise ←

what? you mean I have the _wrong_ kind of chips? →

Carly said not to pay attention to Hilary — she's just like that. Carly was in her class last year and Susie was the one Hilary teased then. I'm just the lucky kid this year.

Hilary has a nose with <u>unusually</u> large noseholes →

"Excuse me, but are you related to a hippopotamus? Your nose has certain similarities."
I always think of things to say too late.

When Hilary kicked the back of my chair, Carly passed me this note:

Just pretend Hilary is a giant cockroach. Then you won't care what she says or does.

It's funny to imagine Hilary as a cockroach, ↗ but it doesn't make the teasing any easier to take.

At recess, Carly and Maya taught me how to jump Double Dutch. I love it! And it's one game where you need <u>3</u> people instead of just 2.

Carly ↘

me →

my shadow has company now ↓

maya ↘

I wore my crown to the alligator town, I sat on a fence and the fence broke down, the alligator bit me by the seat of the pants, and made me do the hootchie-cootchie dance.

Down by the ocean, down by the sea, Johnny broke a bottle and blamed it on me. I told Ma, Ma told Pa. How many lickings did Johnny get?

So I didn't care when Hilary said I jumped like an elephant (well, not much) because Carly invited me over to her house after school! (And she didn't invite Hilary, so there!)

geode

carnelian

green aventurine

ulexite

fool's gold

obsidian

Carly has a cool rock collection →

I love the names of rocks and minerals — like "ulexite." It sounds like a leotard or a small suitcase.

Carly has two big brothers and they're really nice to her. (I'd trade Cleo for either one of them in a second!) They brought us soda and chips in her room. (If I invited Carly to my house, Cleo would steal snacks from us, not offer them to us.)

If I throw in a bowl of chips, would Carly trade a brother for Cleo?

I like Carly a lot, but I don't want to like her too much, because what if she starts liking someone else better, like Leah did?

Carly made me a friendship bracelet like this. I told her about Leah and she says she's not like that.
↓

I thought the worst was over with Hilary, but it's not. Today she passed me a note that was so mean I don't want to write down what it said. Why does she work so hard to make me cry? What did I do to her?

I memorized every inch of this desk

blink, blink blink

me, staring at my desk as hard as I could, so tears would not come out of my eyes

When some people cry, their mouths look like rubber bands.

Some people's chins wrinkle up.

HONK!
Some people sound like they're blowing their noses.

Mom asked why I'm always cranky now, what's going on. I told her about Hilary's note (but I didn't tell her what it said). She hugged me and pulled me onto her lap even though I'm too big for that anymore. She said kids can be mean. I already knew that. Then she told me a story about grandma Sara I'd never heard before. I want to write it down before I forget it.

## Grandma's Story

I never met my grandma, not that I remember, at least. She died when I was little.

But I've seen pictures of her. She looked like this.

When Grandma was a kid, it was the Depression (which was a time when nobody in the country had much money because the banks all failed — they couldn't give people their savings back. That can't happen anymore, but it could then and it was terrible.) She was the oldest of 4 girls and it was really hard for her parents to scrape together money to feed the family.

Her father (my great-grandfather) was an engineer — not the train kind, the building kind. He made bridges before the Depression, but he

people would stand on the street selling pencils or apples or anything they could think of

lost his job (since nobody had money to pay for building anymore), and the only work he could get was being a janitor in a big office building.

from this ↗          to this ↗

He wasn't paid very much, but at least things were very cheap then. Chicken was 29¢ a pound and bread was 10¢ a loaf.

One day Grandma was sent to the store to buy some bread for bread soup because that was all they could afford for dinner that night. Her mother was sick in bed that day, so Grandma had to go.

She held that dime tight, tight, tight, but on the way a mean boy saw her. He knew she had a coin in her fist.

tough mean boy

worried Grandma Sara

hitting fists, not holding fists

tight fist with dime in it

walking fast without running

He followed her and started to call her names,
then he blocked her way and wouldn't let her go any further.

Grandma was scared and ready to cry. She
wanted to throw the money at the boy and run
away. But then she thought of how mad her
mom would be and how sad her sisters would
be with no dinner. The more she thought,
the madder she got, until she was so mad
at this boy — HOW DARE HE DO THIS! —
that she just BLEW UP!

"Who do you think you are to talk to me like that! You let me pass by NOW!!!"

She yelled so loud, people on the street turned to stare and that mean boy got so scared, he was the one to run away.

She felt like when Alice in Wonderland ate the eat-me cake and grew GIGANTIC.

Now he doesn't feel so big and tough.

Mama!

← super soup
(but what is bread soup?
soggy bread in broth?)

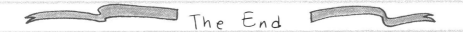

And Grandma said it was the best dinner she'd had in a long time, even if it was only soup.

═══ The End ═══

Mom said Grandma was a lot like me — she even kept a notebook (but she called it a diary). I asked Mom if I could read it, but she's not sure where it is. It's definitely not in our house somewhere, but she thinks Uncle Frank has it. I'm going to write him and ask. It's cool to think that Grandma wrote and drew things just like me. I wonder if she stuck things in her journal like I do. Did she write stories, too?

old photo of Grandma when she was 8 years old →

this is my story, not Grandma's ↓

  The Very Nasty Girl and Her Awful Fate

Once there was this mean girl who no one liked. She got no presents on her birthday because even her parents hated her. (And she had no brothers or sisters because she was so horrible her parents didn't want to risk having another kid like her.)

One day she got a package in the mail. She was so surprised, she opened it right away. It was a box of chocolates, the fancy kind. She stuffed her face with them. Unfortunately for her they were

POISON!

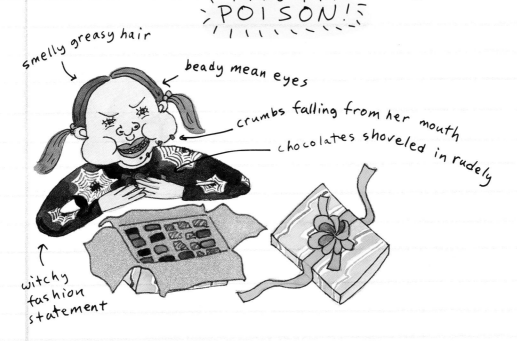

smelly greasy hair

beady mean eyes

crumbs falling from her mouth

chocolates shoveled in rudely

witchy fashion statement

She keeled over and died, and no one bothered to come to her funeral.

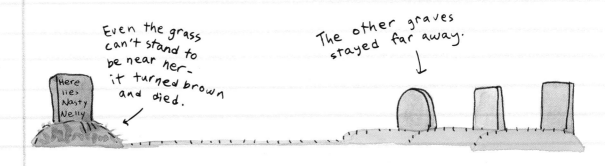

Even the grass can't stand to be near her - it turned brown and died.

Here lies Nasty Nelly

The other graves stayed far away.

Definitely The End

Stories always make me feel better. Even if they don't come true.

Good news! Hilary was absent today. (I hope she has the stomach flu <u>forever</u>.) Then I came home to even better news — a postcard from Nadia!

Dear Amelia,
 Has Hilary turned into a frog yet? Or a cockroach?
 Guess what? I'm going to ~~Space Camp~~ for winter vacation. Ask your mom if you can come, too. It will be great!   yours till the banana splits, Nadia

BLAST OFF!

AMELIA

PESTUS, 27¢
DISGUSTUS
PORTRAIT OF HILARY

564 North Homerest, Oopa, Oregon 97881

Space Camp! I'd **LOVE** to go to Space Camp. How can I get Mom to say yes?

I tried out my angel act on Mom all weekend. I was SUPER nice to her. I did the laundry. I washed the dishes. I dusted. Cleo was astonished. So was Mom.

angel of housecleaning →

sparkling clean dishes

floor clean enough to eat off of ↓

← neatly folded clothes — I even folded the underwear! (even Cleo's !!)

suspicious Cleo →

What's up? There must be <u>something</u> you want.

Mom drinking tea

me, bringing her cookies and the newspaper

Then, when she was all relaxed, drinking the cup of tea I made for her, I asked her about Space Camp.

## AND SHE DIDN'T SAY NO!!

She said, "We'll see." But she smiled when she said it. That means YES in Momspeak, at least it usually does.

Today I didn't even care when Hilary called me lizard face. All I could think about was Space Camp, especially when we launched our rockets. It was waaay cool — and in Space Camp you get to do stuff like that EVERY day.

Carly and I decorated our rocket so it would look really good.

we called it the Saturn 2000 — it was one of the highest. (Hilary's rocket only flew half as far and it broke on re-entry.)

When I got home from school, there was an envelope waiting for me and inside of it was

**Good for One (1) Week at Space Camp (Happy Birthday ~ this is your present)** *very early*

HOORAY!

I called Nadia that night. She is <u>so</u> excited. Me, too! I get to be with Nadia <u>and</u> go to Space Camp!

I can't wait to fly in the simulators!

I want to be head of mission control!

Carly said Congratulations. She wishes she could go, too. Her dad said maybe next year.

I thought Cleo would be jealous, but she says who wants to go to dumb Space Camp anyway? You have to work hard there. She only wants to go to Beach Camp or Camp Make-Up-Your-Face. (She's started to wear gunk on her eyelids so she looks like an alien, but in her case,

Cleo without makeup →

Help! A monster!

Either way, the mirror cracks.

Help! An alien!

Cleo with makeup ↗

it's an improvement.

external fuel tank

solid rocket booster

solid rocket booster

orbiter (what the actual shuttle is called)

I made a calendar to count down the days until Space Camp and I'm reading a book about astronauts and the space shuttle. I hope I get to be the shuttle commander.

T + 2 minutes 5 seconds — solid rocket boosters fall off

T + 8 minutes 50 seconds — fuel tank separates

T + 39 minutes — shuttle in orbit (that's fast!)

Why is it called "T" and not "L" for Lift off? Maybe I'll find out at camp.

T - O - LIFTOFF!

T - 6 seconds - main engines start

T - 2 hours 30 minutes - crew enters orbiter

T - 43 hours - start of countdown

The calendar reminded me I've got to get something for Mako for Christmas. I haven't seen him since last summer at the Grand Canyon, but he's already written me 5 letters (and sent me the good luck charm). Before Carly, he and Nadia were my only friends. (I don't know whether to call Leah a friend or not anymore.) I want to send him something special, something American that he can't get in Japan.

Mako's school photo — he looks just like I remember →

I know what to get Nadia — a rocket
kit like the one Carly and I made. →

Cleo says how do I know Mako celebrates Christmas. OK, maybe he
doesn't, but it sure feels like the whole world does! Anyway I can
always call it a New Year's present. Only what if Japanese New
Year isn't January 1st? Does it really matter? I love getting
presents ANY time of year.

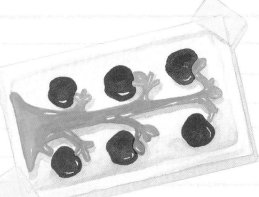

This candy was in the box from
Mako — it looks like fruit
snacks, but it's way too
pretty to eat.

Before I could send
him anything, Mako sent
me a Christmas present
(way early, but that's OK

by me). It turns out he celebrates Christmas
and Japanese holidays, so he gave me a beautiful box
made from a special paper called Washi. Mako made
it himself.

Mako says this is where his family hangs Christmas stockings —
by the bathtub pipe (since they don't have a chimney).

↓

how
cozy!

↑
stockings
hung by the
pipe with care

boy taking
a bath

rubber
duckie ←

Japanese bathtub
(I imagine)

I love reading Mako's descriptions
of his holidays. It makes me want to
go to Japan and see myself.

Mako sent a photo of his sister,
Yumi, dressed up for a November holiday
called Shichigosan — it's like an extra
birthday only a lot more work. (It took
2 hours just to put on her makeup
and get her hair ready.) →

wow — talk about ↑
high heels!

the bow at the back was so heavy, Yumi almost fell over backwards!

My Christmas present to Hilary would be chocolates — _very_ special chocolates.

I still don't know what to get him. Everything here is so ordinary. (And I can't make any thing like a Washi box.)

jelly beans are kind of pretty, but are they special enough?

I like how they look, but hate how they taste.

I got another letter from Mako — already! He was so excited he had to write me about a new donut store. He'd never tasted a donut before! I never would have thought a donut could be special, but I guess it all depends on what you're used to.

Donuts are another thing that look better than they taste.

You can win prizes when you buy donuts — Mako sent me one of his.

Tomorrow I leave for Space Camp and, just in time, I found the PERFECT thing for Mako — it's a notebook, American style, with a set of colored pencils and a bunch of neat erasers. I got the idea from the donuts. Even the most ordinary stuff is different — and cool— when it's from another country. Maybe Mako will send me a Japanese notebook someday. I'd LOVE that.

Mako's new notebook — I copied the recipe for donuts from Mom's cookbook and put it in here along with a copy of the donut song (with pictures, of course).

donut song:
Oh, I ran around the corner and I ran around the block and I ran right into a donut shop and I picked up a donut and I wiped off the grease and I handed the lady a 5-cent-piece. Well, she looked at the nickel and she looked at me and she said, "This nickel's no good to me, there's a hole in the middle and it goes right through," and I said "There's a hole in the donut, too! Thanks for the donut. Bye now!

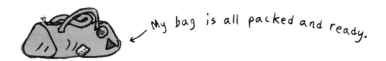
My bag is all packed and ready.

I'm so excited, I can't sleep. Tomorrow I'll be in a dormitory (only at Space Camp, it's called a Habitat). I've never slept in a room with a bunch of strangers before (although I've shared a room with Cleo and she's very strange). I wonder what the showers will be like. And will the food be good or will it be gross cafeteria food? I hope it's astronaut food — that would be cool!

Do astronauts use forks or do they just squeeze food into their mouths?

Dig in!

← astronaut spaghetti

astronaut ice cream →

Every meal comes in little foil pouches so it all looks the same — does it taste the same?

I'm sure I won't miss Cleo, but I'm a little worried about missing Mom — and my room. When we first moved here I hated this room. Now I love it.

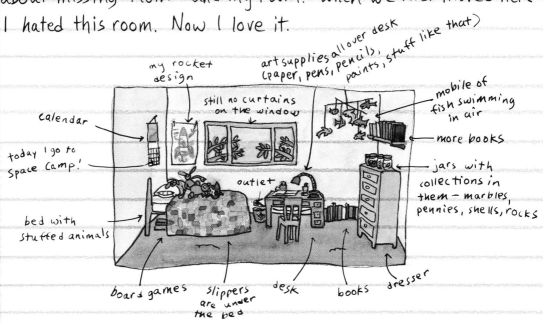

my rocket design

art supplies all over desk (paper, pens, pencils, paints, stuff like that)

still no curtains on the window

mobile of fish swimming in air

calendar

more books

today I go to Space Camp!

jars with collections in them — marbles, pennies, shells, rocks

outlet

bed with stuffed animals

board games

slippers are under the bed

desk

books

dresser

# OFFICIAL SPACE CAMP LOG

Nadia was waiting for me when we got there (it was a loooooong drive — we got up so early it was still night out). I got the bunk next to hers and we're both on Triton team.

So far I'm too excited to get homesick. (But Mom cried when she kissed me goodbye — she said she misses me already and she made me promise to call her EVERY night.)

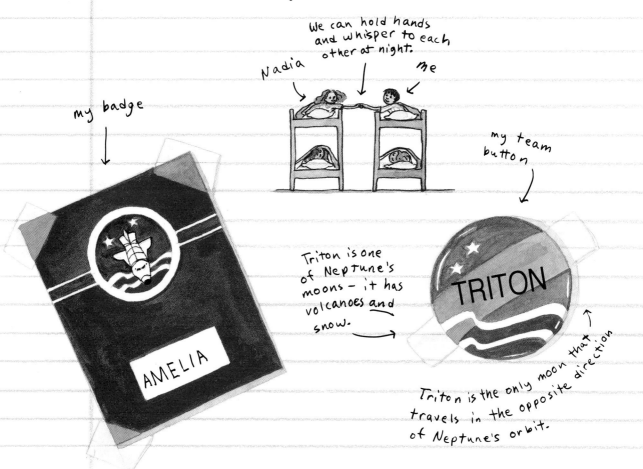

We can hold hands and whisper to each other at night.

Nadia

me

my badge

my team button

Triton is one of Neptune's moons — it has volcanoes and snow.

AMELIA

TRITON

Triton is the only moon that travels in the opposite direction of Neptune's orbit.

space camp pen ↓

We get a pen and a notebook so we can write important stuff down. ↑

We're so busy training, today is the first chance I've had to write in here. (At least I haven't had time to get homesick, either — just a little bit at lunch and dinner because we <u>don't</u> get astronaut food. We get gross cafeteria food <u>three</u> times a day.)

Breakfast is OK. It's hard to ruin cereal and hot chocolate. →

First thing we did was get assigned our positions for flight crew and ground control. Besides Nadia and me, there's only one other girl on our team, Olena. (It's funny, but there are way more boys than girls at Space Camp.) Olena wasn't sure what she wanted to be, but Nadia definitely wanted to be flight director — that's the person in charge of mission control on the ground — and I wanted to be commander, the one in charge of the flight crew. Brad, Evan, and Corey wanted to be commander, too, and they said there was no way I'd get to be commander because I'm a girl and no girl has ever led a shuttle mission.

Not yet, I said.

mission specialist?

payload specialist?

Do I want to be the pilot?

ground control officer?

Olena making up her mind ↑

We had to write down our choices and why we wanted that position. Then we had to answer questions about what we've learned so far. Luther, our counselor, would pick the people with the best answers for each job.

Brad, Evan, and Corey were fighting with each other over which of them would get to be commander — they didn't bother with me because they said there was no way I'd be chosen.

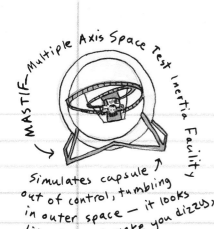

MASTIF - Multiple Axis Space Test Inertia Facility

Simulates capsule out of control, tumbling in outer space — it looks like it would make you dizzy, but it doesn't.

MMU - Manned Maneuvering Unit →

simulates frictionless space you would have in actual MMU — the MMU allows short untethered space walks.

It hovers off the ground - you fly!

We have a _lot_ of training to do to get ready for our shuttle mission. I'll be commander of Discovery. It will be tricky because Luther says something is going to go wrong during our mission (only he won't say what), and we'll have to figure out how to correct the problem.

If we can't solve the problem, we either have to abort the mission (that means cancel it and just return to earth) or we'll crash. Or we might solve it the WRONG way, which means we'll also crash.

Microgravity Simulator — this trains astronauts for moonwalks — you can try different steps. I liked the slow motion jog the best, Nadia liked the bunny hop.

Spinning chair ↓

used to test reaction times after being disoriented by spinning — definitely a barf stimulator for Cleo

NASA loves LAs — that means Long Acronyms, not a city in California.

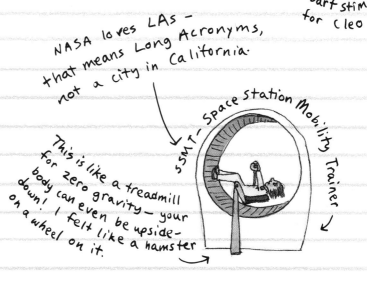

SSMT - Space Station Mobility Trainer

This is like a treadmill for zero gravity — your body can even be upside-down! I felt like a hamster on a wheel on it.

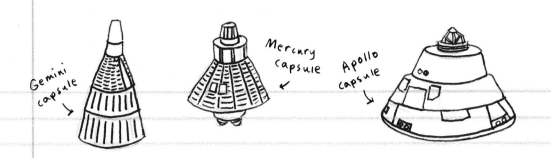

Gemini capsule →

Mercury capsule ↓

Apollo capsule ↓

It's going to be even harder than I thought, because Brad, Corey, and Evan won't listen to me. They say I'm not really commander and they will <u>never</u> take orders from a girl. (But I bet they listen to their moms.) They're ruining <u>everything</u>.

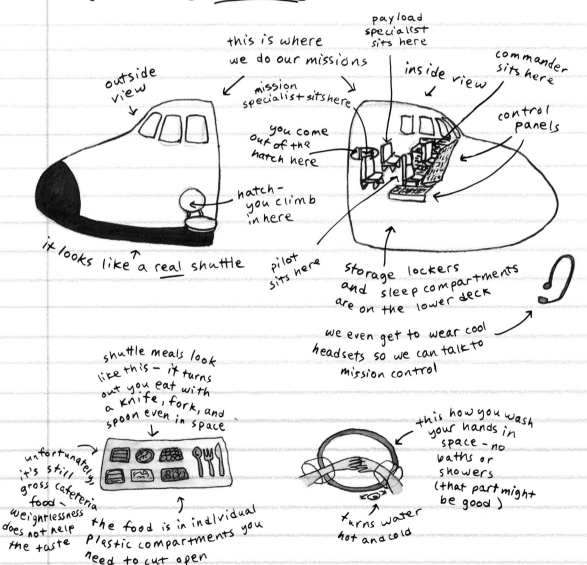

payload specialist sits here

this is where we do our missions

inside view

commander sits here

outside view

mission specialist sits here

control panels

you come out of the hatch here

hatch — you climb in here

it looks like a <u>real</u> shuttle

pilot sits here

storage lockers and sleep compartments are on the lower deck

we even get to wear cool headsets so we can talk to mission control

shuttle meals look like this — it turns out you eat with a knife, fork, and spoon even in space

unfortunately, it's still gross cafeteria food — weightlessness does not help the taste

the food is in individual plastic compartments you need to cut open

this how you wash your hands in space — no baths or showers (that part might be good)

turns water hot and cold

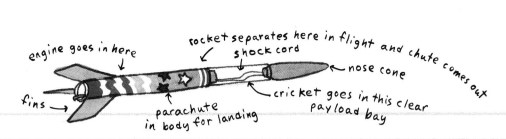

engine goes in here

rocket separates here in flight and chute comes out

shock cord

nose cone

fins →

parachute in body for landing

cricket goes in this clear payload bay

Today we made rockets like Carly and I did at school, only this time there's a clear hollow tube attached to the nose cone. We're going to put a cricket in there and we were supposed to figure out how to build the rocket so that it will launch and land without hurting the cricket.

I hope Evan's rocket crashes into Brad's, whose rocket will splat into Corey's, and they'll all three explode. (Sorry, crickets!)

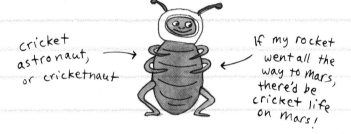

cricket astronaut, or cricketnaut →

← If my rocket went all the way to Mars, there'd be cricket life on Mars!

I called Mom — at last. I know I promised to call everyday, but we're so busy and there's always a looong line at the **pay** phone after dinner. It was great to hear her voice. I even liked talking to Cleo.

You can only talk for 5 minutes, but the line is still loooooooong.

Some kids are really homesick — they don't have a friend here like I have Nadia and they say it's too much. The work is hard, but hard work here. it's the good kind of hard.

my turn at last!

We had a field trip to NASA in the morning. It was really cool. We got to see a real astronaut training in simulators!

Even the bus ride was great – it was the kind of bus with TV sets in it.

After lunch, we launched our rockets. My cricket landed safely! So did Nadia's. Only two crickets fell out when their rockets broke on landing (the parachutes got stuck so instead of gently floating down, they crashed to the ground). One was Olena's, the other was Brad's. (That shows what a rotten commander he would be.)

My cricket didn't make it to Mars, but it got a nice view of Space Camp from high up.

Tomorrow is our shuttle mission and I'm getting really nervous. I heard that Andromeda team blew up on re-entry because the commander forgot to close the payload doors and Callisto team didn't put down the landing gear so they crashed. There's so much to remember! Evan is the pilot, so he's supposed to help me, but I don't know if I can count on him. Brad is payload specialist and Corey is part of ground control so they don't matter as much. At least I have Nadia as flight director. I know I can depend on her.

I've got to sleep so I'll be alert tomorrow.

I keep seeing the control panels in my head, imagining everything that can go wrong.

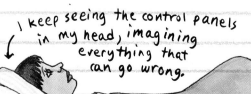

# DISCOVERY MISSION

So much has happened, I'm not sure where to start. We lifted off ok (and it felt _so_ real!). The boosters and fuel tank separated the way they were supposed to, but Evan kept calling me Salamander Amelia instead of Commander Amelia. I got really steamed and that's bad because being mad is distracting and I _had_ to pay attention.

microgravity shoe attachments →

← suction cups anchor your foot to the floor or a workplatform so you don't float around

Even with Evan being a jerk, we deployed a satellite and Olena, the mission specialist, ran her experiments. So far our mission was a success — no mistakes. Then just as we were about to start our deorbit maneuver, an alarm went off — _both_ our orbital maneuvering engines had failed!

Evan went into a total panic. "We're gonna die! We'll be lost in space forever!" He wouldn't stop screaming. Olena was frozen in her chair. I could hear Nadia in mission control saying, "Oh no, oh no."

I wanted to scream

# STAY CALM

but instead my voice got very low and quiet. It didn't even sound like my voice anymore — it was **SHARP** and **HARD** and **GRAY**. All the other kids looked at me with big eyes and Evan stopped screaming.

It was amazing — I felt big and powerful because of that VOICE that you just had to listen to.

Evan

Olena

Brad

I said slowly and calmly, "We're NOT going to panic. We can still land safely." But I wasn't sure how.

Nadia said we could stay in orbit for 15 more minutes, but we had to decide what to do by then. In real life, we could orbit for days. In the simulator, we had to finish by lunch so the next team could go in. Only 15 minutes! That's less time than a math test.

I never thought of voices before, but they really matter a lot.

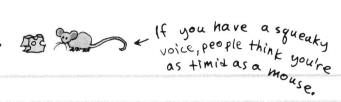

If you have a squeaky voice, people think you're as timid as a mouse.

If you have a cartoony voice, no one takes you seriously.

If you have a scratchy voice, people think you're a witch.

I thought and thought and thought. I tried to remember everything we'd learned. (What kept popping into my head was how to go to the bathroom in space — that was no help.)

Evan, Brad, and Olena kept looking at me, not saying anything, just waiting. Then I had an idea. Maybe if we fired the smaller maneuvering rockets, we could use them instead of the orbital engines to break the orbit and push us back through earth's atmosphere. We'd just have to fire the rockets longer since they were smaller, but how long would be long enough?

Nadia agreed this was our best bet, but I could hear how worried she was →

If you have a croaky voice, people think you're a frog (and they're right!).

No one knew how long we would need to burn the rockets. I would have to guess. Since a regular burn lasts from 2 to 3 minutes, I decided we would try 9 minutes.

We belted ourselves in and Evan fired the rockets. Those were 9 looooooong minutes. I felt like I was holding my breath the whole time.

# IT WORKED!

We landed just fine (I remembered the landing gear, of course), and when we came out of the shuttle, everyone at mission control stood up and applauded.

I felt like a 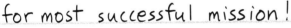hero.

Nadia hugged me. She said she was <u>so</u> proud of me. And for the rest of Space Camp, Brad, Evan, and Corey totally stopped teasing me. Even better, when it was time for graduation, Triton team won the award for most successful mission!

the last day I got to wear my wings

Nadia bought me this patch at the gift shop as a goodbye present — she said I definitely earned it

pin for most successful mission →

It was hard saying goodbye to Nadia, especially since it meant going back to school — and seeing Hilary again. But it feels great to be home (I even gave Cleo a hello kiss —

LANDSCAPE
7¢ POST 7¢

STILL
5¢ LIFE 5¢

10¢ POST 10¢
PORTRAIT

SEASCAPE
3¢ POST 3¢

MODERN
EARTH

she was astonished!)

Mom promised we'd have a celebration dinner of pizza (what I missed the most at Space Camp), but first I wanted to be alone in my room for a while.

I had to say hello to all my old stuff.

↑ familiar lamp

old favorite bear

colored pencils I've made a million drawings with

Going back to school was definitely not easy. I didn't want to go from being a hero to being a jerk (as Hilary calls me).

me walking to school as slowly as possible, all alone again →

Space Camp shirt ←

counting the cracks in the sidewalk to see which comes first — 100 cracks or the gate to school ↘

I'm saving stamps so I can write lots of letters to Nadia (I'm so glad she's still my friend) — and I need to write Mako about Space Camp.

I looked for Carly, but the first thing I saw was Hilary's nasty face, like she was waiting for me.

Well, if it isn't the doofus!

Luckily, the bell rang before she could say anything else.
Unluckily, Ms. Busby gave us a surprise test first thing!

I <u>didn't</u> remember much math. First Hilary, then a math test — it was a rotten day. And it got even worse. At recess, I could see Hilary waiting for me, so I tried to ignore her. But she wouldn't let me.

Hilary's squinty mean eyes ⟶

She grabbed my elbow and said, "I saw you cheating on that test, worm breath — CHEATER!"

Hilary has said <u>lots</u> of mean things to me, but this was <u>the worst</u>. Maybe that's why for once I didn't feel all sad and crumbly inside. I was MAD — I mean, really, REALLY, REALLY

I looked right at her and said in my new SHARP and HARD and GRAY voice,

"You are a lying fink." And once I started, I couldn't stop. It was like all this stuff came bubbling up inside of me and just <u>had</u> to come out.

"You are nasty, NASTY, NASTY. I DID NOT cheat. I don't <u>need</u> to cheat. And there's <u>nothing</u> wrong with my hair or my shoes or my clothes. The only thing wrong with me is that I ever let <u>you</u> bug me. But you're never going to bug me again — you're going to

**BUG OFF!**

Hilary bug

Then I turned and walked away. I wanted to look back and see if she was following me, but I was too afraid to, so I just kept going till I found a tree to hide behind and then I sat down. I was exhausted and empty like I'd run a million miles. Then I felt lighter and lighter, like I could fly (without the shuttle even!).

Carly told me that when I walked away, Hilary started to bawl. She sounded just like a cow!

Hilary all alone on the playground

Carly said she had a rubber band mouth and a crinkly chin.

All the bad stuff I held in bubbled up, out, and awaaay!

I almost felt sorry for her. Almost.

Dear Nadia,
School feels ~~wierd~~ ~~weird~~ ~~wierd~~ aaagh! wierd after Space Camp. But in one BIG way, it's a lot better than before vacation.
Hilary _doesn't tease me anymore_ — it ~~feels~~ GREAT!

Nadia Kury
61 South St.
Barton, CA
91010

yours till saturn rings,
amelia ♡

↑ I wrote my good news to Nadia

More good things that happened today: Carly invited me to sleep over this Saturday, Leah shared her fruit snacks with me at lunch, and Hilary hasn't even _looked_ at me since I told her off. (Why didn't I do that _months_ ago?!)

And the best news is Uncle Frank found my grandma's diary, and he's sending it to me so I can read it. I wonder if the bread soup story is in it.

I guess I didn't need a new hairdo — is this what a commander looks like — me?